To my family for always encouraging me to follow my dreams. —G.G.A.

To Scott, Emily, and Sarah and their families — L.W.K.

For Amelia, Bixby, Stellan, Isaac, Luke, Ezra, Alexa, Grace,
Tobin and the next generation of new readers. – K.M.

STERLING CHILDREN'S BOOKS
New York

An Imprint of Sterling Publishing
1166 Avenue of the Americas
New York, NY 10036

Text © 2016 by Lana Wayne Koehler and Gloria G. Adams
Illustrations © 2016 by Ken Min
Art direction and design by Merideth Harte

ISBN 978-1-4549-1415-0

Distributed in Canada by Sterling Publishing
c/o Canadian Manda Group, 664 Annette Street
Toronto, Ontario, Canada M6S 2C8. Distributed in the United Kingdom by GMC Distribution Services
Castle Place, 166 High Street, Lewes, East Sussex, England BN7 1XU
Distributed in Australia by Capricorn Link (Australia) Pty. Ltd.
P.O. Box 704, Windsor, NSW 2756, Australia

For information about custom editions, special sales, and premium and corporate purchases,
please contact Sterling Special Sales at 800-805-5489 or specialsales@sterlingpublishing.com.

Manufactured in China
Lot #:
2 4 6 8 10 9 7 5 3 1
12/15

www.sterlingpublishing.com/kids

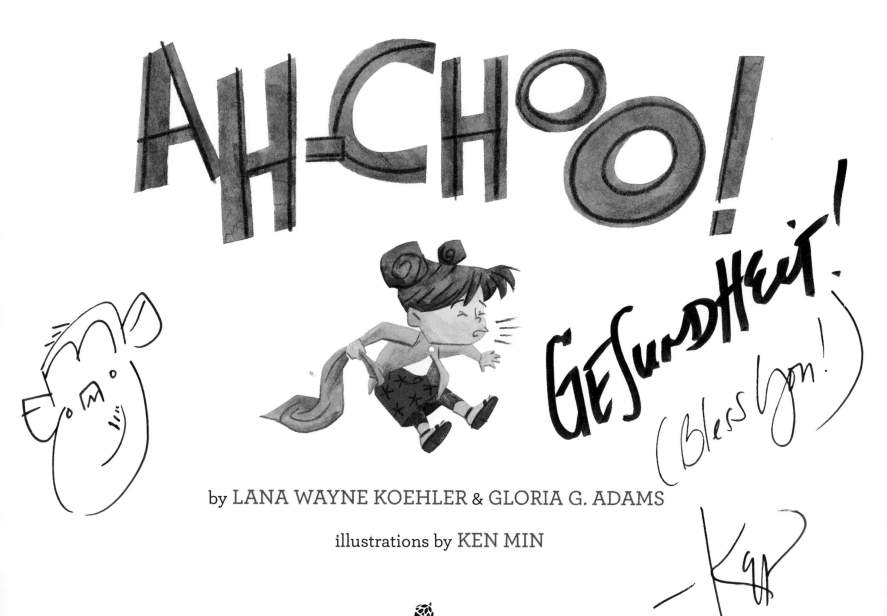

AH-CHOO!

GESUNDHEIT!
(Bless you!)

by LANA WAYNE KOEHLER & GLORIA G. ADAMS

illustrations by KEN MIN

STERLING CHILDREN'S BOOKS
New York

I asked my mom if I could have a pet,
or even two.

But every time I brought one home,
my sister went . . .

At first I tried an Antelope,
and Bobolinks that flew.

But when she tried to pet them both,
my sister went . . .

So next I got a fluffy Cat,
and a Dog from Kathmandu.

But when she snuggled up with them,
my sister went . . .

I tried a feathered Emu,
plus a Ferret, Goose, and Hen . . .

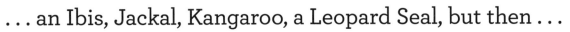

. . . an Ibis, Jackal, Kangaroo, a Leopard Seal, but then . . .

. . . my sister sneezed a bigger sneeze than she had sneezed before.

I took my pets down to the zoo
and went to look for more.

A Monkey and a Nightingale, an Owl that said . . .

"Whoo?"

But Sis let out a mighty wail,
and then she went . . .

The Pig, a Quail, the Rooster who
crowed cock-a-doodle-doo,

a Skunk, and seven silly Squirrels
all made Sis go . . .

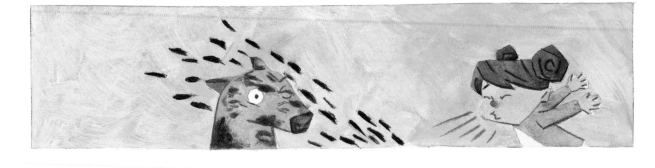

My Takin from the mountain slopes who always liked to chew . . .

...Umbrellabirds,
and Vultures' wings
caused one great big...

A Warthog, Weasel, and a Wolf, a Xantis I named Jack,
a Yaffle and a Zebra, too, I had to take them back.

At last I had a great idea—
much better than before.

I bought a bearded dragon from Mrs. Grey's pet store.

And now we have a brand-new pet.
His name is Mr. Blue.

He's got no feathers, fur, or hair,
so we can hold him, too.

I still can visit my old pets
down at the local zoo.

And best of all, they never
make my sister go . . .